Game Time

The small gym was filling up with spectators, mostly parents and kids from the school. The Palisades players were already at one of the baskets, shooting layups. They looked big and quick. Dunk took a deep breath and started jogging around the perimeter of the court with his teammates.

During the shooting drill, Coach called Dunk and Louie out of the line and over to the bench. "Feeling good?" he asked.

"Yeah."

"Definitely."

"Jared's late, obviously," Coach said. "I don't know when he'll get here, but we've got to make some adjustments."

He looked straight at Dunk and poked him lightly in the chest. "You'll be starting."

ALSO BY RICH WALLACE

Dishes
Losing Is Not an Option
Playing Without the Ball
Restless: A Ghost's Story
Shots on Goal
Wrestling Sturbridge

Winning Season Series
The Roar of the Crowd
Technical Foul
Fast Company
Double Fake
Emergency Quarterback
Southpaw
Dunk Under Pressure
Takedown
Curveball

WINNING SEASON

SECOND-STRING CENTER

RICH WALLACE

PUFFIN BOOKS

PUFFIN BOOKS

Published by the Penguin Group

Penguin Young Readers Group, 345 Hudson Street, New York, New York 10014, U.S.A.

Penguin Group (Canada), 90 Eglinton Avenue East, Suite 700,

Toronto, Ontario, Canada M4P 2Y3 (a division of Pearson Penguin Canada Inc.)

Penguin Books Ltd, 80 Strand, London WC2R 0RL, England

Penguin Ireland, 25 St Stephen's Green, Dublin 2, Ireland

(a division of Penguin Books Ltd)

Penguin Group (Australia), 250 Camberwell Road, Camberwell, Victoria 3124, Australia

(a division of Pearson Australia Group Pty Ltd)

Penguin Books India Pvt Ltd, 11 Community Centre,

Panchsheel Park, New Delhi - 110 017, India

Penguin Group (NZ), 67 Apollo Drive, Rosedale, North Shore 0632, New Zealand

(a division of Pearson New Zealand Ltd)

Penguin Books (South Africa) (Pty) Ltd, 24 Sturdee Avenue,

Rosebank, Johannesburg 2196, South Africa

Registered Offices: Penguin Books Ltd, 80 Strand, London WC2R 0RL, England

First published in the United States of America by Viking,

a division of Penguin Young Readers Group, 2007

Published by Puffin Books, a division of Penguin Young Readers Group, 2008

3 5 7 9 10 8 6 4 2

Copyright © Rich Wallace, 2007

All rights reserved

LIBRARY OF CONGRESS CATALOGING-IN-PUBLICATION DATA

Wallace, Rich.

Second-string center / by Rich Wallace.

p.   cm.— (Winning season ; #10)

Summary: As his own self-confidence grows, seventh-grader Dunk learns
to be supportive both on and off the basketball court when his friend Jared
goes through a difficult time, even though Jared's failure would provide
Dunk more opportunities to prove himself.

ISBN 978-0-670-06150-1 (hardcover)

[1. Basketball—Fiction. 2. Friendship—Fiction. 3. Family problems—Fiction.
4. Self-confidence—Fiction.] I. Title.

PZ7.W15877Sec 2007   [Fic]—dc22   2006038731

Puffin Books ISBN 978-0-14-241216-9

Printed in the United States of America

Set in Caslon 224 Book

FOR SANDRA

• CONTENTS •

I

The Deciding Factor

The late-afternoon wind had turned cold and was right in their faces as a half dozen boys made their way along the Boulevard. Dunk zipped his jacket up to his neck, then noticed that his right shoelace was dragging on the sidewalk.

He stopped and bent down to tie it. Jason Fiorelli, walking a few steps behind, was deep in conversation with Miguel Rivera and nearly tripped over Dunk.

"Sorry, bro," Dunk said.

"No problem, but *whoa*," Fiorelli said. "What size is that shoe?"

"Twelve."

"Yow. That's huge! If you ever grow into those feet, you'll be, like, eight feet tall."

Dunk smiled, placing his hands on the sidewalk and pushing himself up. Four pigeons scattered away.

Dunk's legs were dead tired; Coach Davis had run the players hard today—lots of wind sprints and line drills. "I think I got a blister on my heel. All that scrambling around."

"Get used to it," Fiorelli said. "Coach says he's building this team around *speed*."

Dunk swallowed hard. Speed was one of the major things he lacked. That and jumping ability. "When did he say that?"

"In the hallway yesterday morning. Said he might even go with four guards on the floor some-times with Jared."

"That'd be you, Miguel, Spencer, and Willie?" Dunk asked.

"Probably. He wants to run teams off the court

this season. It's what works best for us. Speed is one thing we got."

"That could be bad news for a big, slow center like me," Dunk said with a frown. He looked away from Jason and stared at the street, busy with trucks and buses and cars. Across the way, the window of Jalapeño's restaurant said AUTHENTIC MEXICANO—FREE EXPRESS DELIVERY.

"Well," Fiorelli said, "you're probably safe. Jared has to have somebody backing him up. He never comes out of the game unless he gets a T, but he got plenty of them last year."

"He had a temper, huh?"

"Yeah, but then he got it under control. Only got kicked out of a couple of games."

Dunk quickly thought over his competition for a spot on the roster of the Hudson City Middle School seventh-grade team. The guys Fiorelli had mentioned were all locks, and he had to figure on Ryan Grimes, Lamont Wilkins, and David Choi making it, too.

That left four spots. There were twenty-seven guys trying out for the team. Only a few of them were slower getting up and down the court than Dunk was.

There was more to it than that, of course. Dunk was the best free-throw shooter in the school, and he'd become a rebounding force and a solid defender. And at five-foot-ten, he was definitely one of the bigger players.

Still, if speed was going to be the deciding factor, Dunk's chances looked a little bleak. Only twelve players would make the roster.

And as much as he loved playing basketball, there was something else at stake, too. Being part of that group—competitive guys like Willie and Miguel; self-assured athletes like Spencer and Lamont; easygoing comedians like Fiorelli and David—that was something Dunk secretly longed for, too. Not for status, but just because they were fun to be around.

The others had kept walking and were now a block ahead of Dunk and Fiorelli.

"You worried that you'll get cut?" Jason asked.

Dunk shrugged. "It's out of my hands. This coach doesn't know me so well. I don't know what he's noticed. And he *did* cut me last year."

Fiorelli, Spencer, and Jared had sparked this group of players to a fifth-and-sixth-grade league championship the winter before under Coach Davis. This year's team would be all seventh-graders, and Coach Davis had moved up to coach them again. He was only in his second year as a teacher and coach, but the players had grown to respect him.

"You have one more tryout session to make him notice," Fiorelli said.

"Well, unless I turn into a track star overnight, I've got nothing more to show."

They walked past Bonita Fashions and El Torito Market. Dunk turned and pushed open the door at Amazing Ray's 99-Cent Store. In smaller letters under the name were the words AND UP.

"Gotta get a new notebook," Dunk said.

"For what?"

"History. I can't believe how many notes we have to take."

"You kidding?" Fiorelli said. "I've only taken, like, six pages all year."

"Then you must have a photogenic memory or something. If I don't write it down, it's gone."

They entered the store and walked past stacks of paper towels and laundry detergent and boxes of cereal and cases of soda. Toward the back of one of the rows, they found the school supplies.

"Here's a good one," said Fiorelli, picking up a notebook with a hot-pink cover and a sticker that said GIRL POWER. "Just your style, Dunk."

"Real funny." Dunk grabbed one that had a New York Giants logo on it, flipped through it to make sure the pages were lined, then looked at the price tag. "This must be one of the 'and up' items," he said. "A dollar fifty-nine."

He found a plain green one for ninety-nine cents instead.

They left the store and spotted Jared Owen walking slowly toward them. Jared was the starting center, a tall, lean kid with quick moves. He and Dunk had been going at each other hard in the tryouts, but there was no ill feeling between them. Both were competitive. And for Dunk, there was a lot at stake: a place on the team.

"What'd you do, stay after practice for extra credit?" Fiorelli asked Jared.

Jared stared at the sidewalk. He looked upset. "Just talking to the coach," he mumbled.

"Must have been some mean talk," Fiorelli said. "What'd he do, ask you to switch to cheerleading?"

"No." Jared practically spit out the word.

"Hey, I'm just kidding around, man."

"Very funny," Jared said. He started walking again, much more quickly.

"Where you rushing off to?"

"What do you think? I'm late for dinner. Aren't you?"

"Maybe," Fiorelli replied. "But it'll keep."

They watched Jared walk off. "Something's bothering him," Dunk said.

"No kidding. He's been like that lately. Moody, you know?"

"Seems okay on the basketball court."

"Maybe, but he's been acting strange off it."

A group of commuters were getting off a bus at the corner as the boys crossed Seventh Street. Dunk and Jason moved to the left to avoid them.

"Maybe Jared's having trouble with his grades," Dunk suggested.

"Nah. He takes even more notes than you do. It's something else."

"Maybe he's got an injury he's not telling us about."

Jason laughed. "No way. He whines about a mosquito bite. Believe me, if he was hurt, we'd all know about it."

"Probably." Whatever it was would pass, Dunk was sure. After all, what could a popular guy like Jared have to worry about? Especially during basketball season.

Dunk had plenty to worry about, though. He was worried that he might not even *have* a basketball season. Tryouts were tough on the nervous system. Made it hard to sleep at night.

Whatever happened, the wait wouldn't be much longer.

2

Cut Day

Dunk carried his sneakers out to the gym the next afternoon and took a seat on the floor, leaning against the wall. A few guys were shooting baskets at the far end of the court. Spencer was on the floor nearby, stretching.

"Lots of scrimmaging today," Spencer said, looking up. He was the starting point guard and a vocal leader of the team.

"Yeah?"

"Yeah. You gotta figure Coach has nine or ten guys already picked, and maybe five or six in contention for the last few spots. So he'll be watching real close what guys can do under game conditions. Guys like *you*."

Dunk took a deep breath and tried to relax, but his heart was already pounding. He'd done all right during the first two days of tryouts, but he was well aware that his performance today would be all-important. Today was cut day. A lot of players would have their hopes crushed.

Coach Davis appeared a few minutes later and blew his whistle. He was tall and thin and looked almost young enough to be in high school. "Let's have five quick laps around the gym, then everyone take a seat in the bleachers," he said.

Dunk had done a lot of running in the fall to get ready for this, so he had no trouble jogging laps. It was the sprints at the end of practice that got to him. In fact, he felt better as he finished the laps than before he had started. More relaxed, now that the sweat had begun to flow.

Dunk had done some counting while the players

were running; there were only eighteen kids in the gym. Maybe Coach had already cut some guys.

"Where is everybody?" Fiorelli asked. "They hiding in the locker room?"

"Everybody's here," Coach said. "Except Jared. He's excused from practice today. The others have been informed that they haven't made the team. . . . No coach likes cutting anyone, but we had more than twice as many kids trying out as we have spots for. So the rest of you are the final contenders. I'm expecting a *lot* of effort out of all of you today."

Dunk did a quick scan of his memory to see who'd been cut. Little Warren Soto was gone, and so was scrawny Mike Cooper. No surprises there. Tarik Howard hadn't made it, but most of the other big men—Dunk's competition at center and forward—were still around.

But where was Jared?

They did passing drills and rebounding drills and shooting drills for an hour, then finally took a three-minute break.

"All right," Coach said, "we're going full-court for the rest of the session, people. I need to see you working out there. *Nobody* has made this team yet."

Dunk let out his breath. Who was Coach kidding? Of course some of these guys had already made the team. Fiorelli, Spencer, Miguel. But Dunk knew *he* wasn't on any list yet.

Coach pointed at Fiorelli and waved him onto the court, handing him the ball. "I want Spencer and Willie out here. You're the guards. Ryan and Fiorelli at forward. Dunk at center. You guys put on the pinnies."

Dunk's mouth dropped open. Coach was putting him in Jared's spot. He stepped down from the bleachers. Fiorelli tossed him a blue-mesh pinnie to put on over his T-shirt.

Coach called five more players onto the floor, including Louie Gonzalez, who'd be matched up at center against Dunk.

Spencer waved the first five over and they huddled up. "Listen. Coach gave me a heads-up before on how he wants this to go. We're gonna run, but he wants us pounding the ball inside *mucho*." Spencer met Dunk's eyes. "He needs to get a handle on the big men before he makes some decisions."

They broke the huddle. Fiorelli put his hand on Dunk's shoulder. "Do it up," he said.

Dunk's sweat suddenly seemed to turn cold, but he took a deep breath and sucked in his stomach. He was nervous. *Just play the game,* he told himself. *Just play some basketball, Cornell Duncan.*

Dunk shook Louie's hand before the scrimmage began. Neither said anything, but they could see what was at stake. There was a good chance that only one of them would be on the final roster. The team probably only needed one second-string center.

Both kids were similar in size and build—tall but on the chunky side—although Dunk had slimmed down a bit since summer. Both of them had close-cropped hair; Dunk's skin was a shade or two darker. He and Louie had been subs on the

YMCA's summer-league all-star team that played in the state tournament down at the Jersey Shore. That had been Dunk's first taste of big-time basketball. But he'd choked with the game on the line in the semifinals.

Dunk had vowed after that tournament to do whatever work was necessary to make the school team this winter. That had included miles of running, hours of solitary shooting at the Y, and even a few of his aunt's evening aerobics classes.

It'd be great if me and Louie both make it, he thought. But this was basketball. No time to be sentimental. All Dunk could do was play his butt off and hope he didn't make too many mistakes.

Spencer wasted no time getting the battle under way. His first pass was to Dunk in the paint. Dunk took the ball and leaned into his opponent, but Louie was a big obstacle to move.

Dunk shifted his right foot as if to step, then pivoted on his left foot and turned to shoot. His jump-hook brought the ball over Louie's outstretched hands, but the ball rattled off the rim and fell toward the floor, where Lamont scooped it up.

Dunk shook his head as he raced up the floor. He reached midcourt and looked around for Louie, who was trailing behind. It wasn't often that Dunk was faster than the man he was covering, but he could definitely outrun Louie.

Louie had a soft touch on his shot, though, and he scored a couple of times before Dunk finally made one. Dunk built a small rebounding edge, however, and he also blocked shots by David and Miguel. He and Louie shoved each other around pretty good, working with everything they had.

After about twenty minutes, Coach pulled Dunk out for a rest. He sat on the bottom row of the wooden bleachers and looked around.

This gym was small and old. The bouncing of the basketball echoed off the gray cinderblock walls. Dunk had been to a few games in this gym as a spectator; it could be an exciting place when the bleachers were full and people were yelling and stamping their feet to spur on the players.

It'd be great to hear them yelling his name some-time, urging him to carry the load as the Hornets battled with a highly touted rival. He'd make the shots, grab the rebounds, stifle their best player with his defense.

When Dunk went back onto the court, he was still matched up against Louie, but now they'd switched sides. Louie was with the starters and Dunk was playing with the backups.

He felt the difference right away. Spencer and Fiorelli and the other first-teamers moved the ball at a crisper pace and were better at setting screens for each other. But Dunk's main concern was stopping Louie, and he managed to do that pretty well while getting a couple of buckets of his own.

So he was feeling good about his chances when the workout ended. He knew he belonged on this team. All he could do was hope Coach saw it that way, too.

Before leaving for the night, Dunk stepped over

to Louie's locker and grabbed his arm. "Nice job today," he said.

"You, too, buddy." Louie grinned broadly and shrugged. "That was quite a battle."

"You said it."

"Hope we'll get to renew it real soon," Louie said. "Like tomorrow at practice would be nice."

Dunk gave a tight smile and nodded. "We'll know soon enough."

"Good luck with it."

3

Sweet as a Lemon

Fourth Street was dark and quiet as Dunk walked past Jefferson Elementary School toward home. A few of the houses still had Halloween decorations, even though it was already late November.

Dunk was starving—it was well past six when he reached his front door.

"Hello, Cornell," his mom called.

"Hey, Mom." Dunk stepped into the kitchen, where his mother was boiling pasta.

"How'd it go?"

"I think it went well. Won't know till tomorrow."

"They're making you wait another day?"

"Yeah. Coach said he'll post the roster in the morning. Guess he didn't want anybody sleeping tonight."

Dunk set his gym bag on the kitchen table. "What are we eating?" he asked.

"I've got chicken in the oven. You can make us a salad." She pointed at the gym bag. "And you can put that stuff right in the washing machine, Mr. Basketball. I found two days' worth of sweaty T-shirts and socks in the hamper this morning, all mashed up and *stinking* wet. You know better than that."

"Yeah," Dunk said sheepishly. "You sure they were *my* socks?"

Mom just gave him an amused stare. Dunk was the only kid in the family.

"Dad home yet?"

"Any second now. He called from downtown about five minutes ago."

Dunk's father worked for the city's department of public works, and his mom was a nurse.

Dunk opened the refrigerator and took out some lettuce and salad dressing. There were two tomatoes on the counter, and he cut them into chunks.

"You wash your hands?" Mom asked.

"I did it at the gym." He opened his palms and held them out. "Not a speck on 'em."

"Aunt Krystal called, too," Mom said. "You need to run over after dinner and feed her cat. She's going to be stuck at school most of the evening."

Mom's younger sister Krystal was a student at St. Peter's University over in Jersey City. She and Dunk were close friends.

The kitchen door opened and Dad came in, rubbing his hands together and smiling. "Smells good in here," he said. He grabbed Dunk and hugged him tight with one arm, then kissed his wife. Mr. Duncan was a big man, always upbeat. "What's the word, Cornell?"

"No word yet."

"Tomorrow," Mrs. Duncan said. "He doesn't find out until tomorrow."

"You'll make it," Dad said. He picked a chunk of tomato out of the bowl and held it up, closing one eye to examine it. "If not, you can get a job as a chef. *Perfectly* cut tomato." He popped it into his mouth.

Dunk rolled his eyes. "Salad. Big deal." Dunk did love participating in the meal preparation, though. He could sauté vegetables and scramble eggs like a pro.

After dinner, Dunk walked back down Fourth Street to his aunt's apartment, on the other side of the Boulevard. Hudson City wasn't a big place—sixteen city blocks long and about as wide, nestled between Jersey City and Hoboken along the Hudson River, directly across from New York City. Dunk had always loved the neighborhood he lived in, quiet and friendly in the midst of such a huge metropolitan area.

His end of town—just a few blocks from the

Jersey City line, was mostly residential. Krystal had a tiny apartment on the second floor of a house, just one big room really, with a small bathroom, and a bay window overlooking the street.

Her little gray cat was sleeping on the sill of the bay window, and it stretched out its front legs and stared at Dunk.

"You hungry, Smoky?" Dunk asked, scratching the cat's chin. "Let's see what we got here."

He shook some dry food into the cat's bowl and looked around.

Aunt Krystal's not much neater than I am, he thought, noticing a blue sweatshirt on the floor, a pile of dishes in the sink, and a damp towel draped over the couch. She taught aerobics at the Y and had been a great athlete in high school.

Dunk's mom had a penchant for neatness. Her little sister hadn't inherited that gene.

"Your mama's running late," Dunk said to the cat, who was still eating. "Uncle Dunk has to pinch-hit today. Don't you worry, she'll be here soon."

Later, as Dunk was getting set to cross the Boulevard, Krystal's car turned the corner and she
beeped the horn as she pulled to the curb.

"Mom said you'd be late!"

"I am late," Krystal said. "Just not as late as I
thought."

"I fed the cat."

"Thanks. Get in."

Dunk opened the passenger door and sat down.

"So he's good?" Krystal asked.

"Who?"

"Smoky."

"Yeah. He's great. We played with his toy mouse."

"Cool. You hungry?"

"Just ate. But yeah."

"I haven't eaten since lunchtime. I'll call your
mom."

Krystal picked up her cell phone from the
console.

"I'm back in town," she said when Dunk's mom
picked up. "Cornell's gonna hang with me for a
while. . . . He will."

"I will what?" Dunk asked.

"Behave."

"Like I don't?"

"I think she means, 'Don't let him eat too much.'"

Krystal drove to the Beijing Kitchen, where she got take-out food at least twice a week. "Let's eat here," she said.

Dunk had been here with Krystal a number of times. The guy at the counter always flirted with her, but she didn't seem to mind.

Krystal ordered something called Double Wonders. Dunk said he'd just have a bowl of egg-drop soup.

"Just soup?" said the guy, making believe that he was shocked. "When I saw you walk in, I told the chef, 'Clear the decks. Get ready for a massive order.'"

Dunk gave a half-smile. "I just ate dinner."

The guy turned toward the kitchen, which was a big open area right behind the counter. He said something in Chinese. Then he turned back to

Dunk with a grin. "I told them not to kill that prize pig yet. Maybe tomorrow."

Dunk laughed. "Maybe."

Dunk was halfway through his soup when he felt a hand on his shoulder. Spencer was leaning toward the counter between Dunk's and Krystal's stools.

"Hey, Spence."

"That looks good," Spencer said, pointing to Krystal's plate. "Shrimp and chicken?"

"Yes. It's delicious."

"Hey, Lin," Spencer called to the counter guy. "Would I like this?"

"I've never seen you not like anything," Lin said. He picked up a large take-out bag and put it on the counter, pushing it toward Spencer.

Spencer handed him some money. "My mom said to make sure we got soy sauce."

Lin opened the bag and peered in. "There's some in there," he said, but he picked up a handful of packets from below the counter and tossed them in.

"Getting cold out," Spencer said. "I should have worn gloves."

"You walking?" Dunk asked.

"What else? It's only six blocks."

Dunk suddenly found some manners. "This is my aunt Krystal," he said.

"Pleased to meet you," Spencer said, sticking out his hand. "I've seen you around."

"I've seen you, too."

"Well," Spencer said, "the family's waiting. Nice job at practice today, Dunk. You were the man out there."

"Thanks."

"What a sweet boy," Krystal said after Spence left.

Dunk laughed. "Sweet as a lemon."

"Oh. One of those?"

"He's a good guy. But that 'pleased to meet you' stuff is an act. Spencer's no gentleman, believe me."

"He seemed mature for a kid your age."

"Sure. Whatever that means. He's all right; he's just got no off switch. Never shuts up, you know?"

"I know the type. But he seems harmless."

"He is." Dunk reached toward Krystal's plate. "You're not going to eat that egg roll, are you?"

"Maybe I am. Maybe I'm not."

"You never eat them."

"You *always* do."

"Why waste it?"

"It's greasy."

"I'll run it off tomorrow. If I make the team, that is."

4

All Elbows

Dunk ran up the steps to the middle school the next morning, eager to check the roster before homeroom. He was even more nervous this morning than he'd been at the tryouts. He couldn't eat his breakfast.

He was early; the school halls were mostly empty. But he could see David and Ryan down at the end of the corridor near the gym, looking at the bulletin board.

The roster was posted there for all to see. Dunk breathed a sigh of relief when he spotted his name third on the list.

Castillo, Alex

Choi, David

Duncan, Cornell

Fiorelli, Jason

Gonzalez, Luis

Grimes, Ryan

Lewis, Spencer

Owen, Jared

Rivera, Miguel

Sanchez, Roberto

Shaw, William

Wilkins, Lamont

Yes! he thought. *All that work was worth it.*

Louie had made it, too. Dunk was glad to see that. There were some better all-around players who hadn't made the cut, but one thing was obvious from the list: this team was guard-heavy. Dunk and Louie added some much-needed bulk to the lineup.

* * *

Dunk hurried out of the locker room after school and up to the court. He wanted to get in some extra shooting before the workout started, but he also wanted to thank Coach Davis for putting him on the roster.

"You earned it," Coach said. "I like how you hustle. But your biggest role on this team will be to keep Jared on his toes. Make him work every single day in practice, for every shot and every rebound."

"Got it." It wasn't quite the role Dunk had been hoping for—he wanted to see significant playing time in the games. But being a bench-warmer was better than getting cut. And he knew that by pushing Jared in the workouts, he would definitely be helping the team progress.

So when Coach lined them up for some five-on-five half-court action, Dunk eagerly set up in a defensive position behind Jared.

The apparent starting five—Spencer at point guard, Willie and Miguel on the wings, Jared at center, and Fiorelli in a floating guard/forward role—

would be on offense the whole time. Coach had
Ryan Grimes covering Fiorelli, Lamont on Miguel,
David Choi on Spencer, and Roberto Sanchez on
Willie.

"Notice anything significant?" Coach asked.

"Yeah," said Fiorelli. "Spencer's got mustard or
something on his chin."

Spencer wiped at his face and looked at a small
yellow smear in his hand. "That's been there since
lunch?" he said in frustration. "Why didn't anybody tell me?"

"It looked good on you," Fiorelli said. "I thought
it was some kind of makeup."

"Thanks a lot, bro."

Coach bounced the ball once and everyone
looked at him. "This is a little more important
than Spencer's grooming. The second line"—he
swept his hand toward Lamont and David and the
others—"are all taller than the starters. Dunk and
Jared being the lone exception. What I'm saying is,
that's going to be a common situation for us this

season. We're fast but small. Most teams are going to out-height us.

"We work the ball around; we look for good shots. We run the fast break when we have the opportunity, and we hustle *every single second* that we're on defense. And despite the general 'shortage,' we have the best big man in the league in Jared. So we *do* pound the ball inside."

Coach handed the ball to Spencer. "Run the offense," he said. "This is not a scrimmage, it's a controlled situation to get the starters thinking like a team. Defenders, when you get control of the ball, pass it back to me and the offense will set up again."

Jared had been quiet all afternoon, but he became vocal as soon as the ball was in play. He shouted for the ball, backing into Dunk to get in position and waving for the pass. Dunk tried to plant his feet, and he kept both hands up, but Jared was big and strong and elusive.

Jared had three baskets before Dunk finally

stopped him, deflecting a shot toward the corner, where Ryan grabbed it for the defenders. Dunk nodded as his floormates yelled, "That's it, Dunk!" and "In his face!"

But Dunk was rubbing his collarbone, which had collided hard with Jared's elbow. In fact, Dunk figured he already had three significant bruises. Jared was putting forth a very physical effort.

Dunk dug in and continued to play hard defense. Jared made some shots, and Coach finally whistled him for an offensive foul when he sent Dunk flying on the seat of his pants. But Dunk managed a few stops and hauled down some rebounds. He was feeling good about his play when Coach brought Louie in to take his place.

After practice, Jared stopped Dunk on the way out of the locker room. "Sorry if I was all elbows out there," he said. "Nothing personal."

"I never thought it was. But the refs will be all over you if you pull that in a game."

"I know. It won't happen. Just had to get it out of my system."

Dunk shrugged. "Well, don't expect me to be a punching bag. I'll give it right back."

"You better."

Dunk nodded toward the door. "You walking home?"

"Of course."

Dunk threw his knapsack over his shoulder and pushed the door open. It was dark out, but the streetlights lit up the blacktop basketball court outside the gym. They walked across it and headed for the Boulevard.

"Good to be back on the court," Jared said. "I would have given anything to be there yesterday."

"What happened?"

"Just some stuff that came up."

"Like what?"

"Nothing good."

"No?"

Jared just shook his head, and they kept walking.

Dunk didn't push it, but he could tell something had Jared shook up. It wasn't like him to take cheap shots at an opponent, especially a teammate. He certainly didn't need to; Jared was bigger, stronger, and more talented than any of the other players.

The wind was in their faces as they turned onto the Boulevard, and it carried a very light drizzle.

"You thirsty or anything?" Dunk asked.

"Definitely. All that running."

They ducked into a small grocery. Dunk picked up a bottle of water and looked at it. He'd dropped several pounds since summer by cutting back on soda, but he wanted a lift after practice. So he grabbed a Coke and vowed that it would be the only one he drank this week.

It was raining a little harder as they stepped back outside. But Jared dropped his gym bag on the sidewalk and leaned against a bench, taking a swig of his drink. He turned and stared up the Boulevard. "You in a hurry to get home?" he asked.

"Pretty much," Dunk replied. "I'm hungry. My parents expect me."

"Yeah. I thought maybe you'd want to stop by the YMCA or something. Shoot some free throws."

Dunk gave a surprised look. "Whew," he said. "I'm worn out from practice. I think I'll pass."

"Okay." Jared picked up his bag and shrugged. "I'll go there anyway." He started walking back toward the Y. "See you tomorrow, I guess."

Dunk watched Jared walk away. Dunk was a gym-rat, too. He spent many hours at the Y, playing pickup games and perfecting his free throws. But enough was enough.

He had the distinct impression that Jared simply didn't want to go home.

5

Juggling Jared

Just one week later, the season got under way. And though the Hornets opened up at home, they couldn't have had a tougher opponent.

Palisades visited the Hudson City gym, looking to atone for a narrow loss to the Hornets in last year's league championship game. Palisades featured lanky point guard Leon "Neon" Johnson, the league's best shooter.

All of the Hornets were aware that Jared had been excused from school for the afternoon, but he was expected to be at the game. But as Dunk put on his uniform in the locker room, it was obvious that Jared hadn't shown up yet.

"Where is he?" Spencer said to no one in particular. Everyone knew who "he" was.

"He said he'd be here," Fiorelli said. "Jared never misses *anything* important. Not sports, anyway."

"Where was he at this afternoon?" Lamont asked. "The dentist or something?"

"He wouldn't say," Fiorelli replied. "Probably that. Probably has to get braces and he didn't want anyone busting on him about it."

"*I* got braces," Lamont said. "So does Willie and Choi and Alex. Who cares? Nobody busts us."

Fiorelli shrugged. "Maybe it's something else then."

"He'd better *get* here," Miguel said. "Palisades is good. They'll eat us up inside if we don't have Jared."

Dunk swallowed hard. He looked at Louie, who looked just as worried. If Jared didn't get here, either Dunk or Louie would take over at center.

"Don't take it as an insult, guys," Miguel said. "But you know what I mean. Neither one of you has Jared's experience."

Dunk checked the clock on the wall above the entrance to the shower room: 3:36. Game time was in less than half an hour. Still plenty of time, but what if Jared didn't show? Would Coach start Dunk?

As if on cue, Coach stuck his head into the locker room. "All right, boys, let's get out there," he said. "Four laps, some stretching, the layup drill, and free throws."

The small gym was filling up with spectators, mostly parents and kids from the school. The Palisades players were already at one of the baskets, shooting layups. They looked big and quick. Dunk took a deep breath and started jogging around the perimeter of the court with his teammates.

During the shooting drill, Coach called Dunk and Louie out of the line and over to the bench. "Feeling good?" he asked.

"Yeah."

"Definitely."

"Jared's late, obviously," Coach said. "I don't know when he'll get here, but we've got to make some adjustments."

He looked straight at Dunk and poked him lightly in the chest. "You'll be starting." He turned to Louie. "And you'll be out there plenty. I'll rotate you two at center until Jared gets here. In and out, like two minutes at a time. We play an up-tempo game, so you'll have to hustle your butts off, come out for a breather, and get right back out there and run."

"Who else is starting?" Louie asked.

"We're going with the small, quick lineup. Spencer, Miguel, Willie, and Fiorelli. Remember, we run the fast break. That's our bread and butter. When you get a defensive rebound, you find the outlet man *immediately* and get up the court."

Both boys nodded. "I'll give you everything I've got," Dunk said, even though he was suddenly feeling ill.

"I know you will. Now go warm up some more."

* * *

Dunk looked around and spotted some of his friends in the bleachers. His parents and aunt had said they expected to arrive by halftime, but they didn't seem to be here yet. *Just as well*, Dunk thought. *This might not be pretty.*

He looked down at his sleek new uniform, the nicest one he'd ever had on.

The red jersey had the number 15 in big bold figures on the front. The knee-length red shorts had wide white stripes down the sides.

Dunk shook the opposing center's hand and stepped into the midcourt circle. The guy was at least an inch taller than Dunk—probably a six-footer—but thinner, with narrow shoulders and big ears. He could jump, though, and he easily tapped the ball to Neon Johnson to start the game. Dunk raced to the paint, putting himself between the basket and his man, number 11.

"Get it inside," called one of the Palisades forwards. They were certainly aware that Jared was not on the court, and figured they could exploit this new guy. Dunk heard the comment. He pressed into his opponent.

And here came Johnson's bounce pass. The center grabbed it and started to dribble, backing into Dunk, who struggled to hold his ground.

The guy stopped his dribble, pivoted left, then swung toward the basket and shot. Dunk jumped and brought his arm down hard, whacking his opponent on the shoulder. The whistle blew as the shot banked off the backboard and into the hoop.

"Yeah, Marty!" shouted Johnson.

The referee pointed to Dunk, then turned to the scorer's table and said, "Foul on number fifteen, red."

Dunk shut his eyes quickly and frowned. Spencer jogged over and put his arm on Dunk's back. "Good pressure," he said. "Keep on him."

Marty sunk the free throw, so Palisades was up, 3–0, after only twelve seconds.

"Right back at 'em," Fiorelli said to Dunk. Spencer was bringing up the ball, shadowed closely by Johnson. Spencer passed to Miguel in the corner. Miguel drove toward the basket, but his path was blocked and Dunk was not in position yet. So Miguel passed back to Spencer.

Dunk sprinted to the basket, breathing hard.

The Hornets' offense was not complicated. The four quicker players passed the ball around the arc, looking for a shot, while Dunk moved in and out of the paint, ready to receive a pass or step up and set a hard screen if one of his teammates drove into the lane. The Palisades center guarded him tightly, keeping a hand between Dunk's shoulder blades.

Fiorelli had the ball in the corner. He pump-faked a shot, and his opponent bought it, leaping to block the ball. Fiorelli squirted past him and bounced the ball to Dunk.

Dunk took it and swung back his arm, pressing into his opponent. Another Palisades player ran over to help out, but Dunk got the shot off anyway as he felt the sting of a wrist against his cheek. The shot missed.

Again came the whistle. The referee picked up the ball and stepped over toward Dunk and the Palisades center. "Let's clean it up," he said. "Too many elbows flying; I'll call those fouls all day."

Dunk walked to the free-throw line. He'd be shooting two. He rubbed his cheek with his fist and waited for the ball.

"Automatic," said Spencer, who was lined up to Dunk's left.

And the first one was—a nice, gentle arc, just over the front of the rim, rippling through the net.

Dunk exhaled hard, letting the air make a whistling sound through his rounded lips. Making that shot was like the sun coming up or something. He immediately felt like he belonged in the game.

The second one was just as true. Dunk ran back on defense.

Johnson and Fiorelli each made a shot, but Dunk didn't touch the ball on the next few possessions. When Miguel got fouled driving for a layup, the horn sounded for a substitution.

Dunk turned and saw Louie jogging onto the court. He walked off, and the spectators gave him a nice hand.

Coach stood by the bench and put his hand atop Dunk's head. "Quick rest," he said.

David squeezed over so Dunk could sit down. And there was Jared, on Dunk's other side.

"Hey," Jared said quietly. "Nice job out there."

"Thanks." Dunk pulled the front of his jersey up and wiped his sweaty face.

Jared was dressed to play. Dunk was surprised Coach had put Louie in. *Guess that's it for me,* he thought.

But when the Hornets called timeout a few minutes later, Coach told Dunk to report back in. Palisades had a 9–6 lead. Coach also put Lamont in for Willie, bringing more size into the lineup. Willie was barely five feet tall. Lamont was a husky five-eight.

"Lamont will move inside with Dunk," Coach said in the huddle. "Go with the three-guard set. And keep running!"

Dunk picked up his second foul, but he later grabbed a rebound and scored after a Fiorelli misfire. So the Hornets had narrowed the gap to 13–12 by the end of the quarter.

Jared took over at center for the rest of the half, but his touch was definitely off. He made only one shot and threw a couple of bad passes. Meanwhile, Johnson got hot for Palisades, helping to build the lead to eight points.

The Hornets were a frustrated bunch when they left the floor at halftime.

Spencer smacked his palm against a locker. "Not in our house!" he said to his teammates. "No way they come in here and embarrass us in our gym."

"Get a grip, Spence," Coach said. "I'm not unhappy with our effort or the execution. The shots just haven't been falling for us."

"We gotta get in Neon's face more," Willie said. "Give that boy open shots and he kills ya."

"True," Coach said. "We'll switch out of our man-to-man defense and go with a box-and-one for the time being. Spencer, you stick with Johnson; Willie and Miguel, you need to collapse in on him a bit and help out. And keep feeding the ball inside to Jared. Those shots will fall soon."

The new defensive set did slow Johnson down, but the Hornets were not able to cut the gap. Palisades was utilizing a similar strategy, having one player glued to Jared and at least one other always in position to double up on him. Jared made a couple of baskets, but he also picked up his second and third fouls.

Midway through the fourth quarter, Coach waved Dunk over to sit next to him. "We need more size out there," he said. "Their big guys are all over Jared—he needs some support under the basket. You report in for Willie, and we'll move Fiorelli out to the third guard spot."

So Dunk checked in. This felt good; this was the real thing. Quality floor time with the game on the line. Dunk turned and saw his parents and Aunt Krystal in the bleachers.

The scoreboard showed 3:46 to play, with Palisades holding a 39–31 lead.

Dunk hadn't played since the first quarter, so he felt a bit out of sync as play began. But he was fresher than the rest of these players, who'd been sprinting and pounding on each other all afternoon. *Be smart,* he thought. *Don't choke.*

Johnson had the ball, crouching low as he dribbled, easily keeping it away from Spencer. He gave a quick stutter to his left, and Spencer stumbled back on his heels. Johnson darted the other way and skipped into the open.

Dunk was guarding a forward near the basket, on the far side from where Johnson was driving. The Palisades center was waving for the ball, locked in a battle for position with Jared.

As Fiorelli stepped in front of Johnson, Dunk

shifted closer to the center, expecting Johnson to pass. And here came the ball. Dunk wasn't quite quick enough to grab it, but he was right there in the action. The center turned toward the baseline, then pivoted back toward the basket, right into Dunk's path.

With a quick swipe, Dunk easily stole the ball and gripped it tightly with both hands. Miguel shouted his name, and Dunk turned and fired an outlet pass. Spencer was already sprinting up the court, five yards ahead of Johnson, and he hauled in Miguel's long pass and made the layup.

Fiorelli's three-pointer a minute later cut the lead to three, but Johnson answered with an off-balance jumper. And when Jared picked up his fourth foul in the final minute, the resulting free throws put the game out of reach for the Hornets.

"If you'd showed up on time, things might have been different," Spencer said sharply to Jared in the locker room.

"It wasn't *my* fault," Jared replied. "Some things

are more important than basketball, you know."

Spencer frowned and took a seat in front of his locker, yanking off a sneaker. "Whatever it was, don't make it a habit."

"Yeah," Lamont said. "Can't you schedule things around the games? Especially a game like Palisades!"

Jared shrugged his shoulders and scowled. "If I could've been here, I would have."

Coach Davis came into the room and leaned against a locker. "Not bad," he said to the dejected players. "Today was their day, but we'll see them again in a few weeks. Spencer, you ran into a machine today in Johnson. And their inside game was better than I'd anticipated. We had some bright spots. Louie and Dunk did a great job filling in underneath. Miguel was sharp. Jared was a little off.

"It's just one loss. It's early. Be here at three thirty tomorrow, ready to work even harder."

Coaches were always saying stuff about every

guy on the roster having an equal role, that the team won or lost together. That was true, Dunk knew it. But being out there at key moments—most of the first quarter and then again with the game on the line—you couldn't beat that.

He peeled off his jersey and wiped his chest with a towel. Coach's bit of praise had softened the sting of the loss a little. Dunk had played an important part in this game.

He left the gym with a large group of players heading uptown, including Spencer, Fiorelli, Lamont, and Jared. Most of them were angry about the loss. They didn't notice that Jared was soon lagging behind.

Dunk waited at the corner of Fourteenth and the Boulevard for Jared to catch up.

"You hurt or something?" Dunk asked.

Jared shook his head and quietly said, "No."

"Just one game," Dunk said. "We'll get 'em next time."

"Yeah."

"Could have gone either way. A shot here, a shot there, and we win it."

"Right."

Dunk wasn't getting much of a response, so he quit trying. They walked the next couple of blocks in silence.

They reached the large digital clock that jutted over the sidewalk from the Hudson City National Bank. Jared stopped and stared at the clock. Dunk looked at Jared, then up. Forty-one degrees at 5:57 P.M. The Boulevard was busy with people going in and out of the restaurants and commuters stepping off the buses and heading home.

"Worst game I've played in a long time," Jared finally said. "I got eaten up by guys I should have smoked. Couldn't make a shot. Couldn't play defense. Fouled everybody who came near me."

"You weren't *that* bad," Dunk said. "You actually kept us in the game."

"Still should have won it. My fault."

Jared leaned against the bank's brick wall, dropping his gym bag to the sidewalk. "You know where I was this afternoon instead of in school?" he asked, not looking at Dunk. "A lawyer's office."

"Why?"

Jared let out his breath, and his mouth fell into a deep frown. "So my parents and their lawyers could argue about where I'm supposed to live while they hack out their divorce. Supposedly they wanted my 'input.'"

Dunk was shocked. He knew kids whose parents were divorced, but he'd never been around anyone while it was happening. He'd never been to Jared's house. He recognized Jared's parents, but he couldn't remember ever speaking to them. "So why are they splitting up?" he asked.

"Who knows? They fight all the time lately."

"About what?"

"I don't know. Money. What we have for dinner. Who does the laundry. Everything, you know? Stuff that wouldn't even matter if they weren't always mad at each other."

Dunk thought about his own home. Just him and his parents, and they all got along well. "So what happened?" he asked. "At the lawyer's?"

"They decided to juggle me back and forth. Most days I'm still here; some days I'm with my dad. He took an apartment over in Hoboken. As long as my mom stays in Hudson City, I can keep going to school here, even if I spend some of my time at my dad's."

"Lots of people go through that, I guess."

Jared shrugged. "I know. Doesn't make it any easier."

"Sure."

"Imagine if I was living full-time in Hoboken?" Jared shook his head and gave a halfhearted smile. "I'd be playing *against* you guys."

"That wouldn't be good."

"Tell me about it. . . . So for now my dad is supposed to pick me up after practice every Wednesday and bring me to Hoboken for the night, then drop me back here Thursday morning. And I'm there every Friday night and most weekends. At least until they work something out for good. If they can't work it out, then a judge decides."

Jared looked away again and wiped his eye. "Don't say nothing," he said softly. "To Spencer and those guys, I mean. I'm not ready to talk about it."

"No problem. Does Coach know about this?"

"Yeah."

They started walking again. They both lived down toward Jersey City, away from the busy downtown area of the Boulevard.

"So why'd you tell me?" Dunk asked.

"I don't know. Everybody knows they can trust you."

"They do?"

"Yeah."

Dunk had never heard that before. It made sense, but it felt good to hear it.

"I feel for you," he said, "but you know I can't go easy on you in practice. That'd make me look bad."

Jared looked surprised. "I don't *want* you to go easier. If anything, go *harder*. That's my oasis out there on the court. You keep pounding me. I'll keep pounding back."

"I plan to."

6

Payoff

Dunk's parents were almost done eating when he got home from the game. There was a plate of fried ham on the table, macaroni and cheese, and a big dish of peas and corn.

"We just couldn't wait any longer," Dad said. "The game ended over an hour ago."

"Yeah. We hung around some after."

"You played great," Mom said. "You want to heat up that ham?"

"Nah, I'm sure it's fine. I'm not too hungry anyway."

Dad looked at his wife with an amused grin. "Not hungry, he says. Just wait—he'll finish every scrap on the table."

Dunk stabbed at a piece of the ham and dumped some vegetables onto his plate. "We'll see."

"You really did play well," Dad said. "I was glad to see Coach put you in during crunch time at the end. Shows that he knows he can rely on you."

"That *was* nice," Dunk said, chewing as he spoke. "Before you got there, I played almost the whole first quarter. Jared was late, so I started."

"Isn't that something?" Mom said. "Sorry we weren't there."

"No problem."

"I'll get off early for one of the games and be there for the beginning," Mom said.

Dunk shrugged. "Today'll probably be the *only* time I start. But yeah, I may see some early playing time. I had four points and I think three rebounds. Plus that steal."

"Well," said Dad, "I promised myself I'd watch the

Rutgers game tonight, and I have just enough time to shower first. You'll clear the table, Cornell."

"No problem."

"You have homework to do?"

"A little. I'll catch the second half of the Rutgers game with you."

"And I have to run over to my sister's," Mom said. "Can you believe that girl doesn't know how to sew on a *button*?"

"Why doesn't she bring it over here?" Dunk asked.

"Lots of studying, she says. I don't mind. I like to get a look at her place once in a while . . . make sure she's not keeping it a pigsty."

Dunk held back a smile. Krystal was in for it, just as Dunk would be if he kept his room a mess.

So Dunk ate the rest of his dinner alone, which suited him fine. He had mixed emotions about the game, but he was barely thinking about that. Jared's news about his parents had him worried.

Everything seemed cool here—his parents almost

never raised their voices, and they seemed like best friends. So he couldn't see them ever breaking up. But he definitely felt bad for Jared.

Dunk did the dishes and climbed the stairs to his room. The house was small—just the kitchen, living room, and a bathroom downstairs, and two bedrooms, an office, and a bathroom upstairs. He shut his door and turned the CD player on softly to an old Tracy Chapman song. Aunt Krystal had loaned him the CD. Then he lay back on the bed and looked around the room.

The third-place medal from last summer's state YMCA tournament sat on his desk. *Should have been gold,* he thought. The coach had unexpectedly put Dunk in the game in the closing minute of the semifinal against Camden, knowing that Camden needed to foul somebody if they had any chance of getting the ball back. Dunk had a reputation for always making his free throws, but he came up empty that time and the game slipped away.

Next to the medal was his only other sports

award—a second-place Little League trophy from a few years before. On the wall above his bed was a Yankees poster from two seasons ago.

Eventually he took his history book out of his knapsack, but after reading the same sentence three times he realized that he wasn't ready to concentrate. So he grabbed last week's *Sports Illustrated* from his bedside table and leafed through that.

Dunk had his window open a few inches despite the cold weather, so he heard his mom's car pull into the driveway a little while later. When he went downstairs, she was sitting on her husband's lap in the big lumpy armchair. Dunk flopped onto the couch. There was a commercial for an insurance company playing on the screen.

"Rutgers up?" Dunk asked.

"Yeah," Dad said. "Second half just started. You finish your homework?"

"Mostly. Not quite. Couldn't concentrate."

"Maybe because you had music on."

"That ain't it." Dunk spread out even more, propping a pillow under his chin. "I was just thinking."

"Well, that's new."

"Real funny."

They watched the game for a few minutes. During the next break, Mom said, "You *are* quiet, Cornell. You upset about the loss?"

"Not so much. Just . . . Jared told me something. . . . He said his parents are getting a divorce."

"That's a real shame." She turned to look at her husband square-on. "Do we know them?"

Dad shook his head. "I don't think so."

"Does he have to move away?"

"Not now," Dunk said. "They're working that out."

"It's too bad," Mom said. "Does he have some close friends?"

"Sort of. Not real close. You know, the guys on the team, like Spencer and Fiorelli and them. But I don't think he hangs out with them much outside of sports."

"Are you close enough to him to help him through it?"

"Maybe. He seems to trust me. . . . He hasn't told anyone else."

"You know what boys are like at that age," Dad said. "Great to joke around with, not real sensitive when somebody has a problem."

"Cornell's different, though," Mom replied. "You're different, Cornell. You can be a great friend, I think. Really give Jared some support."

"That's funny," Dunk said. "Coach said my biggest role on the team is to support Jared. But he was talking about *rebounding*."

"Well, you just be as supportive as you can," Mom said. "Good deeds always get rewarded somewhere along the line."

At bedtime Dunk crawled under his covers and stared at the ceiling. The room never got completely dark; there was a streetlight a few doors down. He gripped his stomach. It was still soft, but the paunch was smaller for sure. He flexed his bicep and felt it with the other hand. The muscle was bigger and firmer. He'd been working hard. Today he'd seen some of the payoff.

He thought through the good things he'd done today: those free throws, some tough defense, the put-back, that steal late in the game.

Even with all that, though, it seemed like the best thing he'd done today was listen.

7

Stepping Up

Dunk pressed his shoulder into Jared's chest, battling to hold his position under the basket. The first-stringers had the ball, and Jared was fighting to get open.

Fiorelli put a move on Ryan and cut toward the basket with the ball. As Ryan scrambled to recover, Jared stepped out to block his path with a screen. It looked as if Fiorelli had a clear path to the basket.

At least it looked like that to everyone but Dunk. He timed his jump just right, reaching for the ball as Fiorelli unleashed the shot.

Smack. The ball soared backward, where Lamont scooped it up for Dunk's side and dribbled quickly toward the opposite basket.

"Dinner," Dunk said with a smile as Fiorelli shook his head and began chasing Lamont. Even during practice, nothing felt as good as coming out of nowhere to send the ball down the other team's throats. That was probably the highest Dunk had jumped in his life.

David scored for Dunk's side before Dunk had reached midcourt, so he hustled back on defense. The second-teamers were giving the starters all they could handle today. The scrimmage was dead-even so far.

"Beautiful," said Louie, who was teamed under the boards with Dunk for the second string. "Show these little guys who's boss."

Coach Davis was big on fundamentals and always spent the first hour or so on drills. But he also wanted the players to have fun, so the second half of practice was often a full-court scrimmage.

That way, all twelve players saw plenty of action.

"You'll spend a lot more time practicing than you will playing the games," Coach had told them, "so you might as well enjoy the workouts."

This time Fiorelli passed the ball inside to Jared, who forced his way toward the basket and shot the ball. Dunk leaped again and his fingers grazed the ball, changing its trajectory just enough to make it miss the basket. And Dunk had Jared boxed out, too, so he was able to grab the loose ball and pass quickly to David.

Dunk's confidence grew with every trip up the court. He made two shots and hauled down some rebounds. Jared scored some buckets, too, but Dunk was matching him point for point.

"You out*played* him today," Fiorelli said as he and Dunk walked home on the Boulevard after practice. "Everybody saw it. You stepped up big-time."

Dunk shrugged. He stopped and reached into his knapsack, taking out a red knit hat and pulling it down over his ears. His head was still damp with sweat, and with the sun already down, the late-afternoon air was very cold.

"Everybody has an off day," he said. "Everybody has a great day once in a while, too."

"Jared hasn't had a good day all season," Fiorelli replied. "Don't know *what's* going on with that boy."

The Hornets had won two games the previous week to raise their record to 2–1, but it had been the play of Spencer and Fiorelli that had been decisive, not Jared. Dunk had seen minimal playing time in the win over Memorial and a few minutes of mop-up duty against Bayonne. Today's scrimmage had been his first significant full-court action in a while.

Dunk changed the subject, sort of. "I felt good today. As soon as I rejected that shot"—he broke into a grin and turned to face Jason—"whose shot was that now? I can't remember. That got me into a different zone. Like it almost wasn't me out there.

Just some other guy named Dunk who was a better player than I am."

"It's all about confidence," Fiorelli said. "You gotta at least *think* you're good, or you got no business being out there on the court. After today, you *better* be thinking you're good."

"Pretty good," Dunk admitted. He knew he'd taken a major step forward as a player. "We'll see what happens tomorrow."

Lincoln would visit the Hudson City gym the following afternoon. Dunk figured he had earned some playing time.

They crossed Twelfth Street and Dunk stopped at the corner. "I'm going into the Y to see my aunt," he said. "You want to come in?"

"Nah. I got a ton of homework. Catch you later."

So Dunk crossed to the other side of the Boulevard and up the steps of the YMCA. Aunt Krystal taught aerobics classes at six and seven thirty on Tuesday nights. It was quarter to six now.

The Y was an old brick building with a small gym

on the main floor and a weight room and lockers below. It was at least as old as the middle school.

Krystal was in a booth off to the side loading the CD player.

"Fast music tonight?" Dunk asked.

"Why? You feel like dancing?" Krystal said.

"I danced big-time in practice today," he said. "The basketball dance."

"That's good." Krystal's white tank top said BER-MUDA, but Dunk didn't think she'd ever been there. "You're not taking my class then?"

"No way." Dunk shook his head. "I'm beat. And we got a big game tomorrow."

"You say that about *every* game."

"That's because it's true! I get psyched for every game. Especially after a day like today."

"You did good, huh?"

"Yeah, I did good."

Several women had entered the gym and were chatting and stretching before class. Dunk waved to one that he recognized from the classes he'd taken in the fall. All that bouncing and kicking and shaking had worn him out, but it had also raised his endurance level. That was paying off now.

"So if you aren't taking the class, then I'm booting you out of here," Krystal said. "No spectators, remember?"

"No problem. Just came in to be friendly."

"Tell your mom I'll stop by after school tomorrow night."

"You won't be at the game?"

"Not on a Wednesday; I've got classes all afternoon. Good luck, though. Kick butt."

Dunk turned and shot an imaginary basketball toward the hoop. He raised both fists in the air and said, "Yes! Game winner."

Back on the street, Dunk walked briskly toward home. A man was walking a golden retriever near St. Joseph's Church, and Dunk stopped to pet it. He inhaled the great smells as he walked past Villa Roma pizzeria and Jalapeños Mexican restaurant. And he glanced in the windows at Amazing Ray's, which were already full of Christmas ornaments and snow shovels and ice scrapers.

And one big thought came to him as he turned the corner onto Fourth Street, better than blocking shots or making baskets or pulling down rebounds. He'd suddenly found some *ups* today. He'd jumped higher than he'd ever jumped in his life. That was an exciting development. Maybe his speed would be next.

8

No More Fear

"**W**hat is this, their high-school varsity?" Spencer whispered to Dunk as the team from Lincoln entered the Hudson City gym. "Those guys must have gotten six inches taller over the summer."

Dunk just said, "Whew. They *are* big."

Lincoln had at least three six-footers, and one of them was pushing six-two. Jared was the Hornets' only six-foot-tall player.

"They're probably not very quick," Spencer said. "We'll run 'em ragged."

"Easy for you to say."

"They don't scare me," said Fiorelli, looking over Spencer's shoulder. "We handled them last year. So what if they're bigger? We're better."

"At least Jared showed up on time for the game for a change," Spencer said, loud enough that Jared could hear it.

"Shut up!" Jared said. "I was late *one* time."

"Yeah, but you've been absent even when you're present half the time," Spencer continued. "You've been invisible most of the games. Or asleep."

"I'll put you to sleep if you don't shut your mouth," Jared said.

Spencer raised his arms and shook his fingers lightly. "Look, I'm shaking with fear."

Jared just shook his head and picked up the basketball.

When the game started, it was clear that the Lincoln team was greatly improved from the previous season, and their size advantage caused all kinds of problems for the Hornets. Coach Davis had stuck with his usual starting five, but that forced Fiorelli and Miguel to cover Lincoln's forwards, and they were having a difficult time. And Jared had picked up two quick fouls trying to protect the inside and support his smaller teammates.

Spencer signaled for a timeout five minutes into the first quarter, with Lincoln ahead, 12–5.

"Dunk," Coach said, "report in for Miguel."

Dunk yanked his warm-up jersey over his head and stepped eagerly to the scorer's table to check in. As he returned to the huddle, Coach gripped him lightly on the forearm. "Take the guy Fiorelli's been covering. Jason, switch to Miguel's man. Jared, lay off those two. Just worry about your man. You can't afford a third foul this early."

Jared nodded. He turned to Dunk. "They crash the boards like nobody we've seen," he said. "Box out and hold your ground."

Dunk sized up his opponent as he walked onto the court. The kid was leaner than Dunk, maybe not as strong, and his two-inch height advantage didn't seem all that significant. But his arms were long and thin, and Dunk had already observed that he was a good jumper.

And even though he'd been playing well in practice, Dunk had that slightly sick, kind of empty feeling he always had when he first entered a game. As if he didn't quite belong out there; that everyone on the court was better than he was.

The guy was all over Dunk as Spencer brought the ball up the court. Dunk decided that his best role might be as a decoy, drawing his defender away from the basket to open up the lane for Jared.

So Dunk stepped outside the key and waved for the ball, but Spencer had passed to Willie. Willie rifled a bounce pass toward Dunk. He grabbed it, but he was outside his comfortable shooting range.

Get the ball inside, Dunk thought. He dribbled once and stopped, but Jared wasn't open either and Dunk's opponent was reaching in for the ball. *Shouldn't have dribbled. Now I've got no options.*

No one was open. Dunk faked a pass back to Willie, then leaped and shot. The ball banged off the rim and the Lincoln center pulled it down.

"Stay inside, Dunk!" Coach called from the sideline.

Dunk stuck close to his man. Coach was right: he was only in the lineup to help out under the boards. He wouldn't do much good fifteen feet from the basket.

So the next time down, he stayed inside, weaving in and out of the key and trying to set a screen for Jared. The Hudson City guards moved the ball quickly around the perimeter as the bigger players tried to get open.

Finally the ball went to Jared. He had good position, but with two fouls already, he seemed uncharacteristically timid. Instead of driving to the hoop, he bounced the ball to Dunk. Dunk grabbed it, pivoted, and laid the ball off the backboard and in.

"*That's* what we need," Coach yelled. "Keep working in there."

And as always seemed to happen, Dunk immediately felt better when he made his first good move, whether it was a rebound, a blocked shot, a layup. He *did* belong out there after all.

Lincoln continued its accurate shooting and led 18–9 after one quarter. Dunk went to the bench and Louie took his place. Lamont subbed for Willie, making the Hornets' lineup a bit taller.

Coach leaned forward on the bench as the second quarter got under way. "Stay alert," he said, looking at Dunk. "You'll be right back in there."

And when Fiorelli got fouled a couple of minutes later, Coach sent Dunk back in for Louie. Lincoln was still ahead by nine.

Fiorelli made the free throws, and Willie made a nice steal in the backcourt, leading to Spencer's layup. The momentum had shifted in a hurry. Suddenly the Lincoln players looked frustrated.

"Our gym!" Spencer called as the Hornets hustled back on defense. "This is our house."

Hudson City eventually whittled the lead down

to three, and the half-full bleachers came to life. "DE-*fense*!" came the cry. "DE-*fense*!"

Dunk was sweating heavily. He leaned into his opponent, keeping him away from the basket, as Spencer and Willie swarmed all over the Lincoln point guard.

The ball flew into the paint; Jared stepped up and blocked the center's path. The shot went up, but Jared was all over it, swatting it out-of-bounds as the Hornet fans cheered.

But then came the whistle. Jared's third foul.

"No!" Jared said, shaking his head in disgust and looking toward the ceiling. "I got all ball."

But the referee had seen it differently. The Lincoln player made both free throws. Hudson City took another timeout.

Dunk looked at the scoreboard: 26–21. Still nearly three minutes until halftime.

"We're switching to a zone," Coach said as they gathered at the bench. "Jared, sit. You can't afford a fourth foul this half. I want Dunk and Louie underneath; Spencer, Miguel, and Jason out front."

Dunk caught Louie's attention and raised his eyebrows slightly. A lot was depending on how the two backups held up under the pressure. Dunk had been playing well, but things would be different with Jared on the bench.

Lincoln did its best to take advantage, pounding the ball inside to the center and forwards.

Fiorelli hit a three-pointer, but Lincoln built the lead back to eight points, then ten.

Time was running out in the half as Spencer brought the ball up one last time. Dunk was panting and sweat was running down his face, but he was ready to expend every ounce of energy he had left.

As the clock wound down, Spencer found Miguel in the corner. The shot looked good, but it rolled around the rim and fell out. The Lincoln center grabbed it and turned, but Dunk swiped it away. He leaned back, jumped, and shot, getting hammered by a pair of Lincoln players as the ball bonked off the rim.

The whistle blew. There was just one second left in the half, but Dunk was going to the free-throw line.

He took a deep breath as the referee handed him the ball. He bent his knees, let out the breath, and calmly sank the first shot.

A cheer went up from the bleachers and the Hornets' bench. Spencer clapped his hands.

Dunk made the second shot.

That was the half. Lincoln 34, Hudson City 26.

"You big guys have to really step up," Spencer said in the locker room.

Coach Davis had already gone over the strategy and pointed out some errors from the first half. He always allowed the captains a few minutes to speak if they wanted to.

"Those guys are huge, and Jared's in foul trouble," Spencer continued. "Dunk and Louie, you heard Coach—you gotta come up big."

Dunk looked down at his size-twelve sneakers.

"Yep," he said softly. He'd wanted a bigger role on this team, and the time was right now. He knew he'd be playing a lot in the second half.

The Hornets started Jared at center, Dunk and Fiorelli at forward, and Willie and Spencer at guard. Fiorelli continued to shoot well, hitting a couple of jumpers, but the Hornets couldn't make a dent in the lead.

The pace was quick, and Dunk was out of breath as the Hornets raced back on defense midway through the quarter. Dunk's man was out in front of him, streaking toward the basket with the ball. Only Jared stood between him and an easy layup.

The guy drove to the hoop as Jared darted over. He made a pump-fake in the air and flipped the ball to the player Jared had been covering. Jared was off balance, but he turned and tried to block the shot. The shot missed, but Jared had picked up his fourth foul. One more and he'd be gone.

The horn blew for a sub, and Lamont came running onto the court. Jared started to walk off, but Lamont shook his head and said, "Coach says you're staying in." He pointed to Dunk. "You're out."

"Quick breather," Coach said, rising from the bench to pat Dunk on the shoulder.

"Jared's got four fouls," Dunk said.

"I know. But we need him out there."

Dunk wiped his face with a towel and looked under the bench for his water bottle. His chest was heaving as he tried to catch his breath. He'd been burned badly on the last fast break, and it had cost Jared another foul.

Dunk's memory flashed back to the previous summer, when he'd been inserted at a crucial time during that tournament semifinal. Hudson City had been beating Camden—the best team in the state. Dunk went in on the theory that he'd get fouled and that would result in some automatic points down the stretch. But it hadn't worked out that way. Dunk had missed three shots out of four while Camden made an amazing comeback.

But today might be different. Just as things were looking bad for the Hornets, the offense came to life. Jared scored on a put-back after Spencer's miss, and Willie stole the inbounds pass and fed Lamont for a layup.

"Dunk!" Coach called. Dunk stuck his head forward and looked at Coach. "Report in for Jared. Cover their center. Let's go!"

A little over a minute remained in the third quarter when Dunk finally got in, and Lincoln held a 47–41 lead. The Lincoln center was four inches taller than Dunk and had strong arms and shoulders. He nodded at Dunk and gave a half-smile as the two players set up under the Lincoln basket. "Get me the ball!" he called to the point guard as Lincoln got set to inbound.

Dunk felt a tap on his shoulder. Lamont was leaning toward him. "My guy can't shoot," he said softly. "I'll be helping you out if the ball comes in."

So Dunk knew he could overplay his man a bit on his right. The Lincoln guards passed the ball back and forth deliberately, looking for an opening.

Dunk clung close to the center, but the guy got loose and the ball came to him just outside the key. Dunk took the chance and blocked the right side. When the center pivoted toward the middle, Lamont was right in his face.

The center shifted back, but Dunk was in his path. He knocked the ball away and Spencer grabbed it. Dunk sprinted up the court.

"Last shot!" came a call from the bench.

Dunk glanced at the clock as it hit twenty seconds. No sense hurrying a shot and giving Lincoln another chance to score before the end of the quarter. Plenty of time to be patient.

But the Lincoln defenders were having none of it, scrambling to make a steal. Spencer's deft ball-handling kept it safe, but he was still outside the arc with eight seconds remaining.

The ball went to Willie in the corner, but a defender was right on him. Willie stepped left then scooted along the baseline. The Lincoln center stepped out to stop him, leaving Dunk alone under the basket.

Willie passed, but the ball was deflected and Dunk had to lunge for it. He grabbed it with both hands, dribbled once, and got hacked as he took the shot.

Dunk stumbled forward and landed on his side under the basket. From that vantage point, he watched as the ball rolled off the rim and out. But he'd be going to the line again.

"Yeah, Dunk!" yelled Spencer.

Fiorelli ran over and gave Dunk a high five.

Dunk sucked in his breath and made both shots. *I'll never choke again,* he told himself.

Though the crowd was small, it sounded like a full house as Hudson City battled its way through the fourth quarter. Each time Lincoln seemed poised to pull away, a Hornet player would make a crucial shot to keep them in it.

Dunk rotated in and out of the lineup with Louie

and managed a three-point play when he got fouled shooting a layup. This time the shot went in, and he added his fifth straight free throw.

But he was on the bench when Hudson City's worst fear came true. Looking to tie the game, Jared drove hard to the hoop and was called for an offensive foul. Less than two minutes remained. Lincoln had a two-point lead and the ball. Jared had fouled out.

Willie called timeout. Jared limped to the bench and sat with his head in his hands. Dunk reported in at center.

Spencer pushed his fist into Dunk's chest. "We need some *stops*!" he said. "DE-*fense*, brother. Don't let that man score."

Dunk did his job the first time down court, sticking to the Lincoln center, who'd had a great game but was clearly tired. Lamont grabbed a rebound after a long miss from outside. He rifled an outlet pass to Fiorelli, who raced across midcourt.

The Hornets were on a three-on-two break, and a

layup would tie the score. But Spencer took a pass at the top of the key, dribbled once, and shot. The three-pointer ripped through the net, and Hudson City had its first lead of the game.

Spencer leaped into the air with both fists raised. Willie and Fiorelli applied pressure in the backcourt; Lamont and Dunk held their ground on defense.

"I'm here," Lamont said to Dunk. "If he gets the ball, I'm with you."

"He" meant Lincoln's center, the most likely target. He'd scored nearly twenty points this after-noon and was the primary reason Jared had fouled out. But he was Dunk's responsibility now.

Lincoln was patient; all they needed was one score. They passed the ball around for most of a minute, then finally bounced it inside. The center took control, and Lamont stepped over to help out. The man remembered what had happened last time he got double-teamed, and he protected the ball as he pivoted and leaped.

Dunk held his spot, firmly planting his feet as the center charged into him. The collision knocked Dunk on his butt. The whistle blew. Offensive foul!

Lincoln was over the foul limit, so Dunk would be shooting free throws.

Lamont stuck out his hand and pulled him to his feet. "Ninety-nine percent!" Lamont said firmly. "You don't ever miss."

Dunk made both shots. He was seven-for-seven from the line today. More important than that, the Hornets had a three-point lead.

Time was moving quickly, and Lincoln needed a big shot to send the game into overtime. With Spencer in his face, the point guard sent a long, arcing shot toward the rim. It hit the back of the iron and bounced high into the air. Lamont slapped at it, and it rolled toward the corner. Willie scooped it up and immediately called timeout.

There were seven seconds on the clock. "Easy decision," Coach said as the Hornets huddled up. "Spencer, pass the ball in. Dunk, get open. They have to foul whoever gets the ball. I want that man to be you."

Lincoln put its center in front of Spencer at the sideline and the quicker forward on Dunk. As Spencer took the ball, Lamont looped around and set a screen, and Dunk stepped out for the ball.

He was immediately fouled as he grabbed it, but the play had been a success. All of Dunk's teammates were standing and hollering. One free throw would seal this game. Dunk would be shooting two.

He'd been in this position before. He'd thought about it all summer and fall.

He shut his eyes quickly, exhaled hard, and made the first shot.

He made the second one, too. When the horn sounded a few seconds later to end the game, the Hornets mobbed him.

The second-string center had come through.

9

The Afterglow

The rowdy locker room felt like a paradise to Dunk. The Hornets had scored a huge come-from-behind victory, and he'd been the fourth-quarter star.

"Thirteen points?" he said in surprise when he heard the statistics. He'd never scored ten before, even in a summer-league game.

"You were the man today," Lamont said, punching him lightly on the arm.

"You, too," Dunk said with a big smile. "Great help defending that big guy."

"Total team effort," Fiorelli was saying. "I mean, our boys come off the bench and knock heads with Lincoln's best. *Totally* outstanding performance."

"I've got something to say," Spencer said loudly, climbing onto a bench and standing with his hands up. "This team is out of sight! Even when our starting center has another terrible game, somebody else steps up and dominates. That's how you win championships. I can't wait until we play Palisades again."

Most of the players cheered. Dunk glanced over at Jared, who didn't look happy. That "terrible" remark had to sting.

No one else seemed to notice that Jared dressed quickly and left the locker room. Dunk was barefoot and still in his uniform shorts, but he pulled on his jacket and stepped outside.

He saw Jared at the edge of the outside basketball court, getting into his father's car. Dunk called his name, but the door slammed shut and the car pulled away.

Dunk stood in the dark with his hands on his hips, his feet ice cold on the blacktop. He stood there for about two minutes, then went inside and got dressed. The rest of the team was still celebrating. Dunk got dressed and left for home.

He decided to avoid the Boulevard, turning up instead to Central Avenue, which ran parallel but was less busy. His warm breath came out in a misty stream, and he tightened the hood of his sweatshirt.

Dunk didn't mind being alone; in fact, he was glad to be. Better to relive what had happened this afternoon, to reexperience the thrill of hitting all those free throws, of making a steal, and playing great defense. And he felt a sudden lifting in his chest as he remembered that first basket he'd made, taking Jared's pass and laying the ball cleanly off the backboard and in. That really was the moment he'd awakened as a ball player. Right then. From that point on, he knew he belonged on the court.

He waited at the corner for some cars to pass, then crossed the street. From this point, the terrain started sloping slightly to his left, then dropped sharply a few blocks away at the cliffs that overlooked the Hudson River. In the near distance he could see the tip of the New York City skyline, all those red and white lights against the clear dark sky.

He'd been walking slowly, enjoying the afterglow of a game well played. But now he picked up his pace, eager to get home.

"Nine for nine?" Dad said when he heard about the free-throw shooting. "That's better than most NBA players!"

"Yeah, well, I don't do that *every* game," Dunk said, digging into his plate of chicken and rice. "Actually, I'm eleven-for-eleven on the season, though. Had two in the first game."

"Better not jinx it, Cornell," Dad said with a laugh. "They say if you talk about a perfect streak, you'll ruin in."

"I thought that was a baseball superstition," Mom said.

"It holds true in any sport," Dad replied.

"I make close to ninety percent in practice, but a game is a different story. You're out of breath; everybody's watching. I was just in a groove today."

"Confidence," Dad said.

"That, too."

The back door opened and Aunt Krystal walked in. "How'd you do?" she asked Dunk.

"Not bad."

"You guys won?"

"Yeah. Big comeback."

"You get in?"

"A little." Dunk broke into a silly grin.

Krystal gave her sister a questioning look, then turned back to Dunk. "What?" she asked.

"What do you mean?" he said.

"You're hiding something. I can tell by that smile."

"I was high scorer. Jared got in foul trouble and

I ended up playing a ton. I had thirteen points."

"Whew! Must be those aerobics classes you took last fall."

"That helped."

"Helped? You wouldn't have lasted three minutes without 'em."

Krystal pulled out the empty kitchen chair and sat down. "Can you spare some food for a poor, starving college student?" she asked.

"Help yourself," Mom replied. "Maybe we all can go out for dessert after. Celebrate Cornell's big day."

"Where to?" Dunk asked.

"The doughnut place or something. You earned it."

"Yeah, I did." Dunk caught Krystal's eye. "I'll do some extra sit-ups tomorrow. Tonight I'm eating what I want."

10

Teamwork

The next day's practice started in an upbeat way, with lots of sharp passes and chatter from the players. But it wasn't long before they noticed how quiet and serious Jared was acting.

"Hey, we *won* yesterday," Spencer said to him at one point as they stood in line during a layup drill. "We're on a roll, bro. Smile."

Jared turned and faced him, but he just gently rolled his eyes and looked away. The ball was passed to him, and he drove to the hoop, cleanly making the shot.

"Jared's got the blues!" Lamont cried.

"He's as blue as a blueberry," said David.

Spencer clapped his hands, waiting for the next pass. "Fundamentals!" he said with fake enthusiasm. "We *love* to work on fundamentals."

Dunk had to laugh at that one. Coach had been setting up one drill after another—shooting, rebounding, passing. They'd been at it for more than an hour. It wasn't much fun.

Finally Coach blew his whistle and had the players sit in the bleachers. "Yes, we're on a roll," he said, "but let's not get *too* confident. Yesterday was a great team effort. Monday we play at South Bergen. They're undefeated, and they beat Palisades earlier this week. So nobody's etching our names on the championship trophy just yet."

He set them up for a full-court scrimmage, with Dunk at center opposite Jared. They walked onto the court together, but Jared kept his eyes on the floor, a light scowl on his face.

Must still be angry about yesterday, Dunk

thought. *But he's got no reason to be mad at* me.

Whatever Jared was angry about, it was Dunk who took the punishment. Not that Jared played dirty, but he seemed more focused than ever and determined to dominate the scrimmage. He scored two layups and a short jumper in the first few minutes, blocked one of Dunk's shots, and grabbed two rebounds.

Spencer kept up his usual verbal barrage, encouraging all of his teammates and shouting, "Yeah, Jared!" after a couple of plays. But Jared held his stern expression and never said a word.

Lamont started to sing in a flat monotone. "He's got the basketball blues."

A couple of others joined in. "The basketball *blues.* . . ."

Dunk sat on the bottom row of the bleachers a while later and watched as Jared outplayed Louie even worse than he'd hammered Dunk. He scored on four consecutive possessions, but he never once broke a smile. He didn't show any emotion;

in fact, just kept hammering away and scoring.

"Come on, Stone Face!" Spencer said. "At least *pretend* to enjoy it."

Coach stopped the slaughter a few minutes later and had Jared take a break. Jared walked past Dunk on his way to the water fountain.

"Incredible job," Dunk said.

Jared kept walking. But he came right back and sat next to Dunk, leaning on the second row and letting out his breath. "'Bout time," he said.

Dunk nodded slowly. "'Bout time is right."

"You played great yesterday, Dunk."

"Thanks. You weren't so bad, either, you know."

"I stunk. I've stunk all season. . . . Yesterday was the low point."

"If it was the low point, that means you're on the upswing now."

Jared smacked both hands lightly against his thighs. "Seems that way . . . You've been kicking my butt out there."

"Not today I wasn't."

"Yeah, well . . . those other days."

"I think you made up for it today."

Jared looked a little embarrassed. He gave a half-smile. "I haven't made up for anything until I start performing in the games. But I think I'm ready now."

"Everything else okay?"

Jared shrugged. "Okay, I suppose. My parents stopped fighting, I think. I mean, they can't much, since they don't live in the same house anymore."

"I guess that's good."

"I had a long talk with my dad last night. He convinced me to block that stuff out when I'm playing. Or, not block it out entirely, but feed off it. Take control where I can. Stop being 'terrible.'"

"Spencer didn't mean nothing by that," Dunk said. "He just runs off at the mouth."

"No kidding. I gotta hand it to him—he never stops."

"You can't let it get to you."

"I know. I let that happen last year. This is different. I *have* been playing badly. None of these other guys know that I had a legitimate reason."

"So . . . you spent last night in Hoboken?"

"Yeah," Jared said. "Most of my stuff is at my mom's, so the apartment's kind of spare. I have a radio in my room and a couple of magazines. I don't know anybody over there, so I just hang out with my dad and watch TV. It's sort of fun, actually. He was always working so much that we never spent much time one-on-one, just the two of us."

Coach Davis's whistle made them both look up. "We've got fifteen minutes," he said. "I want the five biggest guys out here on one side: Dunk, Lamont, Jared, Louie, and Ryan. The other seven will rotate for the opposition. See if speed can overcome height."

And though the speed made a difference, no one was able to contain Jared. With Dunk and Louie offering support, Jared continued to roll up big points.

Spencer eventually appointed himself center for

the smaller team, moving inside and sticking close to Jared. Spencer had some strength and was very quick, and he did a decent job of slowing Jared down. That left Louie and Dunk to take up the slack, and they both responded with buckets.

Jared gripped Spencer's hand as the scrimmage ended. "Good job," he said softly.

"You, too," Spencer replied. "Nice to see you back from your nap."

"Nice to *be* back finally."

Saturday afternoon Dunk got a call from Spencer.

"Team dinner, if you're up for it," Spence said. "We're meeting at Villa Roma around four thirty for pizza and stuff. You in?"

"Think so."

"That'll make six of us. Jared's mom says he's in *Hoboken*. I don't know where Fiorelli or Lamont are. You seen 'em?"

"No." Dunk hadn't left the house all day.

"Anyway," Spencer said, "bring money if you come."

"Yeah. Four thirty at Villa Roma."

"Right. I still gotta call a few more guys."

"See you then."

Dunk checked with his parents, then went upstairs to take a shower. It occurred to him that he was still the only one on the team who knew *why* Jared would be in Hoboken on a Saturday. But it wasn't his place to say anything. Jared would reveal that on his own.

"Ten bucks enough?" Dad asked.

"I would think so," Dunk said. "Should be plenty."

"Here's twelve. Figure three or four slices, a drink."

"You're awesome, Dad."

"Hey, it's important to hang out with your friends. Have a great time. And leave a tip."

Dunk tucked the money into his pocket and walked downtown.

Villa Roma was a popular hangout for Hudson City athletes. The middle-schoolers knew they needed to get there in the afternoon because the high-school kids would take the place over in the evening. The main room had two big-screen TVs that were usually tuned to sports, plus there were video games and the pizza was inexpensive.

Dunk took a seat at a round table with Spencer, Ryan, David, Miguel, and Louie. There were two pitchers of soda on the table.

"Willie's showing up later," Spencer said. "Maybe Roberto, too."

"You order?" Dunk asked.

"Two pies. One with peppers. We'll get more if we need to."

The talk was mostly about the basketball season. Miguel had heard that South Bergen had a new guard who was at least as good as Palisades's Neon Johnson.

"He doesn't scare me; I'm up to it," Spencer said. "And if Jared's got his head back together, we'll have no trouble. Suddenly we're looking *big*. The way my man Dunk's been playing gives us some real force inside."

"What's he doing in Hoboken anyway?" Miguel asked. "Jared, I mean."

"Maybe he's got a girlfriend," David said. "He hasn't been hanging out with us at *all* this season."

"Doubt it," Spencer said. "In Hoboken? How would he meet somebody like that?"

David shrugged. "Who knows?"

"He's visiting a relative," Dunk said. As soon as he'd said it, he wished he hadn't.

"How do you know?" Spencer asked.

"He mentioned something. I don't know. . . . He said something after practice."

"He's the mystery man," Miguel said. "Disappearing Jared."

"As long as he doesn't disappear from any more games," Spencer said. "We can't have that boy fouling out. That could kill us."

"Didn't kill us the other day," Miguel said.

"Yeah, but it would."

Willie came into the restaurant then, and the talk quickly changed. He'd just had his hair cut extremely short, making his ears appear to be jutting out even farther than usual.

Miguel whistled. "Whoa, what did you do, run into a buzz saw or something?"

Willie gave an embarrassed smile. "The guy went a little nuts, huh? I told him *short*, but I didn't mean bald."

"It'll grow back," Dunk said, rubbing his own short hair. "It's a cool look, anyway."

"It's *severe*," Spencer said. "Here comes the food."

A waitress set a pizza on the table, and all seven boys grabbed for a slice. When she returned with the second pie, Spencer said, "Better make us another one, please. These'll go *fast*."

The talk turned to school and girls and more about basketball. Dunk didn't say much, but he sure felt good to be there. A full-fledged member of the team.

11

Opportunities Taken

Monday's bus ride to South Bergen took the team along the Hudson River and up past the Lincoln Tunnel. The ride was stop-and-go, with lots of traffic lights. Dunk sat near the back and looked out the window.

Jared came back after a while and took the seat next to him. "I told those guys what's been going on," he said. "I'm not using it as an excuse, but . . . it's been a distraction, to say the least."

"Today's a new day."

"Can't wait. Big game, too."

"Huge."

Dunk took a deep breath as the bus pulled into the South Bergen parking lot. Coach had told him he'd be first man off the bench today. "Expect a lot of playing time," he'd said before they boarded the bus.

Jared fell into step with Dunk as they walked toward the gym. "My dad says he's going to look for an apartment in Hudson City after the first of the year," he said. "So my whole 'commuting' back and forth might be over soon."

"That'd be a relief, huh?"

"Definitely."

Dunk felt great warming up: loose and quick. *Fast* almost. It was as if his whole body had changed in the past few months, becoming much more athletic and coordinated. There was more to it than that, though. His whole outlook had changed, too. He was confident.

So when he entered the game midway through

the first quarter, that frightened, nauseated feeling from the other games was no longer there. Instead, he couldn't wait to get involved.

Hudson City was up by a point and had the ball. Spencer shot from outside, and the ball banged off the rim. Dunk timed his jump well and got a hand on the ball, but he couldn't bring it down. It fell to the floor. Jared grabbed it on the first bounce and laid it off the backboard and in.

Dunk turned and found the forward who'd been covering him and ran up beside him as they made their way toward the opposite basket. The guy was quick and had scored twice with Fiorelli covering him, but Dunk stuck with him. He got position under the basket and kept his man away.

South Bergen missed a shot and Dunk turned to box out. Jared grabbed the rebound, hit Miguel with the outlet pass, and watched as Willie took the second pass and drove in for a layup.

Twice more Hudson City made defensive stops, and twice more they raced up the court for layups.

South Bergen called for a timeout. The Hornets had a seven-point lead, and the packed gym was quiet.

"We're running them ragged," Spencer said in the huddle. "They can't penetrate with all that bulk we've got underneath, and we're totally in their faces outside."

"Good run," Coach Davis said. "Keep it up. These guys have the potential to score a lot of points in a hurry, so maintain the pressure."

By halftime, the Hornets had a double-digit lead, and Jared had already scored eleven points. Dunk hadn't scored, but he'd played several minutes in the second quarter and had been a factor.

"It makes a big difference when you're in there," Jared said as they walked out of the locker room for the second half. "They double up on me when we've got the smaller lineup on the floor. They can't do that if you're playing."

Dunk nodded. He stood a little taller and pushed his shoulders back. Circumstances had certainly

gone in his favor so far this season. Jared's occa-
sional absence and frequent poor play had given
Dunk the chance to show his stuff, and he had
done well in those instances. That had led to the
present situation, where Jared was back in business but Dunk's value had also been established.
He'd capitalized on his opportunities.

And he knew that the reason he'd been able to
capitalize was the work he'd put in prior to the season. All that shooting and drilling on his own, all
those pickup games at the Y, all that running. He'd
made his own luck; he'd worked for it.

So when he reentered the game in the third
quarter, it was as more than a second-string bench-
warmer. He was a key member of the Hornets. And
the Hornets were looking like a first-place bunch
again.

The lead was nearly twenty points when Dunk
went to the free-throw line late in the fourth quarter. He hadn't scored at all today, but he'd done his
job in other ways.

None of the Hudson City starters were still in the game. Jared, Spencer, Fiorelli, Willie, and Miguel were on the bench now, enjoying the final minutes of a romp.

Dunk took the ball from the referee and dribbled it twice. He bent his knees slightly, drove his shoulders up, and unleashed the ball in a perfect arc. It swished through the net, and his Hornet teammates cheered.

"One hundred percent!" yelled Lamont, who was tensed on the line, waiting to battle for a rebound.

Dunk thought for a second. *Twelve for twelve on the season. Not too shabby.*

He allowed himself a smile. Dribbled twice. Bent his knees. Shot the ball.

Bonk.

The ball hit the back of the rim and bounced out. In the scramble for the rebound, it rolled out-of-bounds.

The horn blew for a substitution. Louie ran onto the court with a grin, pointing at Dunk.

Dunk stood with his hands on his hips for a second, then walked toward the bench. The starters all stood and clapped. Spencer embraced him, and Jared whacked him on the shoulder.

"Overconfident!" Willie said with a laugh.

"Never," Dunk said. "Never *under*-confident again, either."

"Thought you'd never miss another one," Miguel said in mock surprise.

Dunk shook his head and smiled as he took a seat between Jared and Spencer. "I won't miss many," he said. "But I guarantee I'll be making a lot of them. For many seasons to come."